Help! Shark! Help!

Suddenly something brushed against Rose's leg. Normally she would have kept her cool head and figured it was a hunk of seaweed or a small fish. But now just one thing entered her mind: Shark! A maneating shark had her number and was closing in for dinner!

"I felt him!" she screamed. "Shark! Help! Shark!"

Alkali's face went white as paste. All he wanted to do was to get to the beach, and get there fast.

Arms flailing like windmills, the pair cut through the water. They'd never swum so fast or been so scared.

Me and my stupid treasure, Alkali thought grimly. We're done for, and all for a few gold coins.

THE CASE OF THE SLIPPERY SHARKS

by Stephen Mooser

Illustrated by Leslie Morrill

Troll Associates

This book is for Matthew and Thatcher Weldon
and all the other students
at my alma mater, Del Mar Elementary,
Fresno, California.

Library of Congress Cataloging in Publication Data

Mooser, Stephen.
    The case of the slippery sharks.

    (Treasure hounds)
    Summary: Three friends interested in searching for
treasure become involved in searching for stolen goods.
    [1. Mystery and detective stories] I. Morrill,
Leslie H., ill. II. Title. III. Series. IV. Series:
Mooser, Stephen. Treasure hounds.
PZ7.M78817Cas   1988   [Fic]   87-3490
ISBN 0-8167-1177-1 (lib. bdg.)
ISBN 0-8167-1178-X (pbk.)

A TROLL BOOK, published by Troll Associates,
Mahwah, NJ 07430

Contents

1

Sand Treasures

EARLY ONE SUMMER MORNING, while most of the little seaside town of Shadow Beach was still asleep, the Treasure Hounds—Rose Flint, Stanley Duggins, and Alkali Jones—pedaled their bikes down to the beach to search for treasure.

The beach, which had been crowded the day before, was empty now, save for a flock of sandpipers scurrying in and out of the surf. Overhead, high above the tall cliffs that rose from the beach, seagulls were squawking, but the birds themselves were invisible, hidden behind a low, clammy fog that smelled of salt water and seaweed, and chilled the air.

"I wish I'd brought a sweater," said Alkali. He pulled his cowboy hat down around his ears, then wrapped his arms around his chest. "Brrrr! And I wish this fog would burn off."

"I wish I'd just stayed in bed," added Stanley. "The beach this time of day gives me the creeps. In the movies, it's a foggy morning just like this when big ugly sea monsters come crawling out of the surf and start eating people."

Rose rolled her big green eyes and clucked. "Stanley, in case you haven't noticed, this is real life, not the movies. Besides, it's a scientific fact that monsters don't exist."

"Oh, yeah?" said Stanley, a tall, gangly boy whose face was plastered with freckles. He placed his hands on his hips. "What about the Loch Ness monster? Tell me it's not real."

"It's not," said Rose. "There isn't a shred of scientific evidence that proves it exists."

"I don't know," said Alkali. "I've seen pictures."

"Alvy, pictures can be faked," said Rose.

"Please, Rose, the name is Alkali, not Alvy. How many times have I told you that?"

At least a thousand times, thought Rose, and she was probably pretty close. For the last year Alvy had been insisting that his friends call him Alkali, after the name of a famous old prospector, Alkali Jones, whom he'd read about in the pages of his favorite magazine, *True Treasure*.

Stanley cast a wary eye toward the surf. "Look, are we going to hunt for treasure, or not? I don't want to be here all day."

Rose flicked on a swtich at the base of the long-handled metal detector she'd brought to the beach, and said, "All right, let's see what we can find."

Slowly fanning the detector over the sand, Rose waited for the clicking sounds that would tell her metal was buried nearby. The Treasure Hounds had actually found a lot of stuff that summer, including a bunch of water-logged watches, three rings (none with diamonds in them), and nearly fifty dollars in change.

Of course, when possible, they worked for others. They had a regular business helping people find things that had been lost. Already they'd had jobs looking for rings, a buried jar of coins, and, once, even a missing safe.

Click-click-clickety-click-click. Rose's detector suddenly sprang to life. No doubt about it. Treasure was not far away.

A big fat gold ring covered with rubies and sapphires, thought Rose.

A pile of gold coins, wished Stanley silently.

"A pop-top off a can of juice," announced Alkali, holding up the bit of metal he'd pulled out from under the detector. He shook his head. "Sometimes this beach is worse than a junk yard. It's as bad as this Idaho mining town I read about, Vienna, Idaho. People are still trying to find a silver hoard they believe is buried there. But they can't because of all the junk metal left years ago by miners."

"I wish people weren't such litterbugs," said Rose as she returned to her detecting.

Nevertheless, the Hounds soon hit pay dirt, finding sixty-five cents in coins buried just an inch beneath the surface.

While Rose and Alkali scoured the sands for coins and rings, Stanley patrolled along the cliffs at the back of the beach. The surf had piled up all kinds of things against the rocks, and he enjoyed picking through the mess, looking for anything of value. Among the bottles and cans, the sandals and the seaweed, the driftwood and the scraps of plastic, he'd sometimes find a special treasure. Once he uncovered a wet, but still usable, ticket to a Flaming Cranes rock concert. Another time, he discovered a perfectly good set of binoculars. And on another occasion, he came across a stuffed, mounted owl. He was particularly happy to be searching along the cliffs this morning, because it was as far away as he could get from any monsters that might be lurking about in the fog-shrouded surf.

Suddenly, something shiny and white, partially hidden behind a torn sandal, caught Stanley's attention. Piece of marble, he guessed, or maybe even a shark's tooth.

To Stanley's surprise and horror, what he had found was not a solitary shark's tooth, but what looked like a complete set of human dentures!

"Awwk!" he screamed, making a leap that just might have earned him a world's record for the backward jump. "It's a— it's a—it's a—"

"Stanley!" said Rose. "It's a what?"

"A sk—sk—sk—"

"Stanley! Spit it out!" Alkali ordered.

Stanley gulped and continued backing away. "A sk—sk—skull!" he stammered. "Over there!"

Rose's eyes widened; Alkali's, too.

"I'm serious," said Stanley, motioning toward the driftwood. "Go look. See for yourself."

Rose and Alkali glanced at the driftwood, then at each other. Neither moved.

"Stanley," said Rose, narrowing her eyes, "are you positive?"

Stanley raised his hand. "I swear that's just what

I saw. A human skull. I wouldn't kid about something like that."

Alkali and Rose exchanged another fearful look, then started slowly for the spot where Stanley had pointed.

"Look under that sandal," said Stanley, still keeping his distance. "You can't miss it."

Alkali drew in a deep breath and leaned over the woodpile cautiously, as if expecting to find it crawling with rattlesnakes. Rose bent over, too. Brushing a wisp of red hair out of her eyes, she couldn't see anything at first. Then, squinting, she caught sight of a pair of smiling choppers buried in the sand, screeched, and nearly leaped out of her shoes.

But Alkali didn't flinch. That was because he didn't see a skull. All he saw were teeth.

"Is this your skull?" he said, reaching into the woodpile.

"Oh, my," said Rose when she saw what he had found, "it's not a skull at all, only a set of teeth carved out of a piece of bone."

"Probably whalebone," said Alkali. He turned the six-inch-long carving over in his hands. "Do you think some sailor was trying to make himself a set of false teeth?"

"No sailor did this," said Rose. She pointed to a line of triangles, circles, and stars that ran along the top of the bone. "These are Indian symbols."

"What makes you think that?" asked Stanley.

"We've been studying Indians in school," said Rose. "My teacher, Mrs. Hartz, says that Indians

lived in caves all along this coast. She even taught us how to read some of their writing."

"So what does it say?" asked Stanley.

"I don't know for sure," said Rose, "but I think it's some kind of a good luck piece." She pointed to a cluster of stars in one corner. "This was the local Indians' symbol for prosperity."

"Do you think it's valuable?" asked Stanley.

"Maybe," said Rose, "but don't count on its bringing you good luck."

"Why not?" asked Stanley.

Rose clucked and shook her head. "Because good luck charms don't bring good luck," she said. "It's a fact that things like four-leaf clovers and rabbits' feet don't bring good luck. That is just a bunch of superstition."

"Yeah, well I don't agree," said Stanley. He held the teeth up near his face and wagged them back and forth, pretending to make them talk. "Stanley is soon to become very rich, thanks to me. Sorry, Rose, you're going to be out of luck for not believing in my powers."

They all laughed. Stanley slipped the teeth into the back pocket of his jeans, and Alkali said, "Watch out you don't get bitten." And they laughed again.

The rest of the morning flew by.

They found another four dollars and thirty-seven cents in coins, two sets of keys, and a silver ring featuring a curled snake with fake ruby eyes. But the biggest find of the morning wasn't made by Rose's detector. Just as they were getting ready to pack up for the day, Alkali spotted a sliver of gold poking out of the sand. When he scooped up the object, he was surprised to discover that he'd found a gold coin.

"Look at this!" he exclaimed. He gaped at the heavy coin in the palm of his hand and saw the thin outline of a cross surrounded by some crude writing. "It's a doubloon!"

"A doubloon?" said Stanley.

"An old Spanish coin," said Alkali. "Pirates used to carry around chests full of these things."

"Pirates!" said Rose.

Alkali licked at his lips and stared out to sea. "Remember the big storm that hit here last week?" he asked.

"Sure," said Stanley. "What about it?"

"Storms can sometimes uncover old wrecks lying at the bottom of the ocean," said Alkali. He squinted as if he were trying to see beneath the water. "The storm could have washed this coin ashore."

Rose raised her eyebrows. "Then maybe there could be more of these out beyond the surf."

Alkali rubbed his hands together and turned to Stanley and Rose. His eyes were gleaming. "This could be just like the *Whidah!*" he said excitedly.

"'Widda?'" Stanley repeated. He plucked the coin from Alkali's hand and held it up to the light. "What in the world is a 'widda'?"

"The *Whidah* was a pirate ship under the command of Sam Bellamy," explained Alkali. "She was wrecked in a storm, and her cargo washed up on the beach. People who lived near the shore collected a treasure from her every time the tide came in."

"This could be the break we've been waiting for,"

said Rose. She clapped her hands together. "Wow! A real pirate treasure!"

"All we have to do is get our snorkels, fins, and masks, and search the bottom of the ocean," said Alkali. "That wreck, if it's there, shouldn't be hard to spot."

"And you shouldn't be hard to spot either—by sharks," said Stanley. "It's summertime, remember, and the waters are warm, perfect for sharks."

"There hasn't been a shark attack around here in years," said Alkali. "Stanley, you're the biggest worrywart I've ever known. What's wrong? Did you see *Jaws* last night, or something?"

"This has nothing to do with *Jaws*," said Stanley. "Didn't you see the story in the paper yesterday— about that kid in Florida?"

"Stanley, this isn't Florida," said Rose. "Anyway, we'll be careful."

Stanley handed the coin back to Alkali and shook his head. "Go on, get eaten for all I care. To me, though, it doesn't seem worth the risk. Not for a little bit of gold."

Alkali tossed the coin into the air, caught it, then closed his hand tightly around it. "We're not talking about a little bit of gold, my friend. We're talking about tons of it—millions and millions of dollars' worth!"

Alkali looked as if he were ready to jump into the ocean and start searching right then and there. But Rose, as usual, kept a cooler head.

"Before we do anything, we'd better make sure our doubloon is real," she said.

"How can we do that?" asked Stanley.

"We'll go to that new place on Main Street, the Hammerhead Art Appraisers," said Rose. "They're supposed to be experts on the value of anything old. They must know what a doubloon looks like."

Alkali opened his fist and stared down at the gleaming coin. "Are you going to make us rich?" he asked.

"There's only one way to find out," said Rose. "Head for the Hammerhead Art Appraisers."

2

Trouble in Town

THE NEXT DAY, on the way to the Hammerhead Art Appraisers, the Hounds stopped by Rose's house. Since it was nearly noon, Rose's mother sat them down in the Flints' sunny kitchen and served lunch, melted cheese sandwiches.

"We discovered a doubloon on the beach," said Alkali.

"That's very nice, dear," said Rose's mother, a thin, rosy-cheeked woman with her daughter's red hair. "I've always thought doubloons are such pretty birds."

"No, no, Mrs. Flint," said Alkali, taking the gold coin from his pocket, "a doubloon isn't a bird. It's an old Spanish coin. Here, take a look at it."

Mrs. Flint walked to the table and examined the coin in Alkali's hands. "Oh, my," she said, "is this real gold?"

"We hope so," said Rose. "We're going down to the Hammerhead Art Appraisers to let them look at it."

"Hammerhead? Hammerhead?" said Mrs. Flint, furrowing her brow. "Is that the place on Main Street?"

"That's the one," said Rose. "We've heard they are experts at telling people what their valuables are worth."

"We're hoping they'll tell us it's real," said Alkali. "If they do, we're going to look for more."

"Mrs. Flint?" said Stanley, who hadn't been paying the least bit of attention to the conversation. Instead he'd been staring out the window and gulping down his lunch. "Are there any more sandwiches?"

Mrs. Flint smiled. "Stanley, I don't understand how you stay so thin," she said. "You eat like a herd of starving horses."

"I'm a growing boy," said Stanley. He shrugged his shoulders. "I can't help it, I guess."

"Of course I'll get you another sandwich," said Mrs. Flint. She smiled at Rose and Alkali. "Anyone else?"

"No, thanks," said Rose.

"We really should be going," said Alkali.

"The sandwich will only take a second," said Mrs. Flint.

"And another second after that for Stanley to eat it," said Rose. She looked out the window. "Anyway, I don't think—" Stopping in midsentence, she put a hand to her mouth and gasped.

"Rose!" said Mrs. Flint, alarmed. "What is it?"

Rose's eyes were wide as saucers. She pointed out the window. "It's Mr. Drabb from across the street. Look, he's—he's gone crazy!"

"Oh, my," said Mrs. Flint, hurrying to the window, "he looks as if he's trying to tear out his hair."

He certainly did. Mr. Drabb, who was wearing a

rumpled tuxedo, was pulling on his long hair with both hands and running around in circles, like some wind-up toy gone berserk.

"What's he doing in that outfit?" asked Stanley. "Is he a waiter?"

"Maybe he's on his way to a prom," suggested Alkali. .

"No, no, Mr. Drabb is a musician with the symphony," explained Mrs. Flint. "He must be playing somewhere today."

"We'd better go see what's wrong," said Rose. She grabbed the rest of her sandwich from her plate and got to her feet. "It looks like Mr. Drabb needs our help."

"He isn't dangerous, is he?" asked Stanley.

"Of course not," said Rose, starting for the door. "Hurry, before it's too late."

The Treasure Hounds, with Mrs. Flint close behind, dashed out of the house and crossed the street. By the time they reached Mr. Drabb, he'd calmed down a little and was sitting on top of one of the metal garbage cans on the sidewalk in front of his house. His head was in his hands, and he was mumbling something to himself, though no one could quite figure out what it was.

"Mr. Drabb," said Rose, tapping her neighbor on the shoulder, "are you all right?"

Mr. Drabb looked up. His hair stuck out wildly, like porcupine quills, and his bloodshot eyes were as red as tomato juice.

"My cymbals, my precious cymbals," he cried, "they've been stolen."

"Stolen!" said Mrs. Flint. She looked hastily around, as if the thief might still be lurking about.

"Those were the finest cymbals in the whole wide world," cried Mr. Drabb. "They were once owned by Vladimir Von Pratt, the greatest cymbalist in history."

"Von Pratt?" said Alkali. "I think I've heard of him."

"Everyone's heard of him," said Mr. Drabb. "Though he played the cymbals over a hundred years ago, he's still famous today. His grand finales were spectacular. Stupendous!"

"Then those cymbals you lost must be very valuable," said Stanley.

"They were priceless," moaned Mr. Drabb. He shook his head. "But that's not the worst of it."

"It isn't?" said Rose.

"Hardly," said Mr. Drabb. "Would you believe I've got a concert in just half an hour, and without those cymbals there can be no grand finale," he cried. "Who could have done such a thing?"

Mrs. Flint shook her head and put a hand on Mr. Drabb's shoulder. "It's terrible what's been happening in this town the last few months," she said. "It seems as though there has been a robbery almost every day."

Mrs. Flint wasn't too far wrong. Over the last few months, the town of Shadow Beach had been plagued by a series of robberies. People had lost all kinds of valuables to the thieves. Silver, jewelry, even paintings had recently been reported stolen. Unfortunately, the police didn't have a clue as to who the robbers were. And now, poor Mr. Drabb had become the latest victim of the crime wave.

"In a few weeks I was going to retire and pass those cymbals on to my son," said Mr. Drabb. He looked as though he might burst into tears at any moment. "Now, not only are they gone, but the concert is ruined."

"What you need to do is call the police," said Alkali.

"It wouldn't do me any good at this point. The concert is in half an hour," said Mr. Drabb. He jumped off the garbage can. "Let's face it. Today's symphony will have to be called off."

"Maybe you can buy some cymbals," said Rose hopefully.

"Where do you suggest I go?" said Mr. Drabb. "The nearest store with a decent set of cymbals is miles away."

"How about borrowing some?" asked Stanley.

Mr. Drabb shook his head at the suggestion, but not Mrs. Flint. To her it made perfect sense. She snapped her fingers, turned, and without a word, ran back to her house.

"What's wrong with your mother?" asked Alkali.

"I don't know," said Rose, watching as her mother disappeared into the house. "Maybe she forgot something cooking on the stove."

Mr. Drabb looked up into the clear blue sky and sighed. "I wonder what Von Pratt would have done in a situation like this?"

As Mr. Drabb contemplated the possibilities, Mrs.

Flint emerged from the house. In her hands she held a pair of small silver cymbals.

"Yoo-hoo!" she called, hurrying across the street. "Look at what I found. The cymbals Rose used to play in kindergarten when she was five."

"Oh, Mother," said Rose, embarrassed, "those are for little kids. Mr. Drabb doesn't want toy cymbals. He needs real ones."

Mr. Drabb smiled at Rose, then reached for the cymbals. "What I need right now is something I can play at the concert," he said. "Let's give these a try."

Mr. Drabb took the little cymbals in his hands, lifted them over his head, and clanged them together.

"Hmmmm," he said. "The tone leaves a lot to be desired, but—"

"But it's better than calling off the concert," finished Mrs. Flint.

"You're certainly right about that," said Mr. Drabb. He clapped the cymbals together again, this time even harder than before. Even though they were toys, in the hands of a professional like Mr. Drabb, they sounded almost authentic.

"That's not too bad," said Rose.

Mr. Drabb banged them together again, and the sound improved still more. "Perhaps these will do," he said. "I just hope the conductor understands."

"I'm sure it will be a first for the symphony," said Mrs. Flint.

"Of that there is no doubt," said Mr. Drabb. He looked down at the tiny silver cymbals and shook his head. "I hope these will be loud enough for the grand finale."

"At least there's going to be a grand finale," said Rose.

Mr. Drabb gave Mrs. Flint a big smile. "I can't thank you enough. I do believe you've saved this afternoon's concert."

Mrs. Flint beamed at the compliment. "Maybe my daughter and her friends can help you track down your real cymbals," she said.

"We're the Treasure Hounds," said Stanley proudly.

"We'll keep our eyes open," said Alkali. He glanced up at the sun. "But right now, I'm afraid we have to be heading for town. We're going to the Hammerhead Art Appraisers."

"Hammerhead? They're good people," said Mr. Drabb. "They just did some work for me. I found them quite reliable."

"That's good to hear," said Alkali. "We're counting on them to start us off down the road to riches."

Mr. Drabb smiled and waved farewell with the cymbals. "Thanks again!" he shouted as they departed. "I hope you find that road."

3

The Dead Spider and Captain Jib

THE HAMMERHEAD ART APPRAISERS was housed in a narrow office between the Shadow Beach Beauty Parlor and the Kingsbury Insurance Agency. The office itself was totally unfurnished save for a wooden counter at the rear of the room and some posters advertising vacations in Greece, left over from the last tenant, the Sunshine Travel Agency.

When the Hounds first walked in, they saw a fat lady in a polka-dot dress talking to a man and a woman behind the counter. Standing against the side wall and holding a large tan cloth bag was Captain Jib, one of Shadow Beach's most famous citizens. A plump, big-nosed man with a gray beard and a scar across one cheek, he looked as fearsome as any movie pirate, but, in reality, he was a gentle man who rarely raised his voice, and then only when really angered. Many years before he'd sailed the seas, captaining freighters all over the world. Now retired, he watched those same kinds of freighters through his long telescope, which he kept out on the deck of his cliffside home.

The Hounds nodded politely to Captain Jib and went up to the counter, where the fat lady had just removed the lid from a big silver box and was showing the contents to the art appraisers standing before her.

The male appraiser was a short man with slicked-back hair and black brows that formed a sharp V above his eyes. He looked as though he was about to gag.

"Where did you get that awful thing?" he asked.

His partner, a tall woman with a beehive hairdo and bright red lipstick, looked into the box and started to laugh.

"Why, it's just like one of those things on *Invasion of the Mutants*," she said. She looked up at the fat lady. "This thing real?"

The lady turned the box over, and onto the counter spilled a giant red and purple spider the size of a fist.

The Hounds gasped and stepped back in perfect unison.

The fat lady turned and smiled sweetly. "Don't worry, children. He hasn't been alive for years. My late husband captured him some time ago in the jungles of South America."

Alkali forced a smile and tried to think of something nice to say. "That sure is one big spider," he said.

"The biggest in the world," said the lady. "And the rarest. This is the only one that's ever been found." She turned back to the appraisers. "Well, what do you think it's worth?"

The man shook his head and stepped away from the counter. "You say it's rare?"

"Quite," said the woman.

"I don't know," said the man. "A museum might pay you something for it, but I doubt it." He looked at his partner. "What do you think, Dixie?"

Dixie smiled. "I'm afraid the market for dead spiders is currently at rock bottom. Do you have it stored in a good place?"

"Oh, yes," said the woman. "I keep it on the top shelf in my hall closet. The temperature there always stays the same, and as long as it's in the box, moths can't get to it."

"Good," said Dixie. "I suggest you hold on to it for a few more years, till the market turns around. Sell it then."

The woman carefully placed the spider back in its box and shut the lid. Then she gave the pair behind the counter a few dollars and thanked them for their time. "With all the robberies we've been having lately here in Shadow Beach, I worry about my valuables," she said. "That's why I thought this might be a good time to sell."

"I understand," said Dixie sympathetically. She patted the woman's hand. "The thieves have us all worried."

After the woman left the store with the spider, Captain Jib stepped up and placed his cloth sack on the counter.

"Captain Jib!" said the man. "One of our favorite customers. It's always a pleasure to see you, sir."

The captain reached over the counter and shook

the man's hand. "Aye, good to see you, Garth." He smiled at the woman. "You, too, Dixie. I want you to give me your opinion of a little something I picked up forty years ago in the wilds of New Guinea. If you place a high enough price on it, I'm going to offer it for sale."

Garth reached for the sack. "Very well, let's see what you have here."

"Avast! Not so fast, lad," said Captain Jib, suddenly yanking away the sack. "The thing in here isn't your ordinary South Seas souvenir. It comes with a curse, a powerful one at that." The captain narrowed his eyes and stared long and hard at Garth. "Do you believe in magic spells?"

Garth clicked his tongue and rolled his eyes. "Of course not," he said.

The captain turned to the Hounds. "What about you? Are you afraid of the evil eye?"

Stanley gulped. He didn't know what the evil eye was, but he did know it didn't sound like anything to mess with. However, before he could say a word, Rose answered for them all.

"Of course we don't," she said. "It's a scientific fact that curses are just a bunch of baloney. Everyone knows that."

The captain raised an eyebrow and looked at Rose. "All right," he said, "take your chances, folks. Open the sack, Garth."

Captain Jib must have been a strong believer in the evil eye, because he turned his back before the sack was opened. He never saw what was inside, but everyone else did. And what a sight it was! The thing that Garth drew out of the sack was a skull made of solid jade and nearly as big as a bowling ball. Most amazing of all was a giant ruby, as big as a cherry, that was set into the center of the thing's forehead.

'Wow!" said Alkali.

"That's got to be worth a fortune!" exclaimed Rose. "Where did you say you got it? New Guinea?"

"It cost me half a year's pay," said the captain, his back still turned. "But for some reason I couldn't resist it. Only later did I learn that anyone who stared into its evil eye would be cursed by bad luck."

Stanley gasped and quickly turned away. Even Alkali lowered his eyes. But not Rose. She'd never heard such rubbish.

"I bet some art museum would love to have this," she said.

"And they can have it," said the captain, "if Garth and Dixie here tell me it's worth enough to sell."

Dixie and Garth passed the head back and forth, examining it carefully.

"This is a pretty piece," said Dixie, at last. "But I think you'd be wise to hold it another two months. There's going to be an auction of South Seas art in New York later this fall. We'll notify you when it comes up. Sell it then, and you'll get your best price."

Captain Jib folded his arms across his chest. "I respect your advice, mates," he said. "Put it back in the sack, and I'll take it to New York in the fall."

Garth did as he was told, and the captain turned around again.

"I hope you're keeping this in a secure place," said Dixie, handing him the sack.

Captain Jib winked. "Don't you worry. My treasure's as safe as the gold in Fort Knox, kept under lock and key in my old sea trunk, it is. It's a stout old chest, believe me."

Dixie smiled. "I don't doubt that, Captain Jib. I can see you're a man who protects his goods, and protects them well."

Captain Jib snorted his agreement and was about to turn away when he saw Alkali take out the gold coin he'd found on the beach and lay it on the counter. "Why, what have you there, lad? A doubloon?"

Alkali nodded. "I think so. We just found it yesterday morning."

Captain Jib picked up the coin, turned it over in his hand, then put it in the corner of his mouth and bit it.

"That's quite a piece," said Garth. "Where did a boy like you happen to come by such an unusual coin?"

"Why, I found it, sir—on the beach," said Alkali.

"The beach?" said Dixie.

"Sure," said Stanley proudly. "We're the Treasure Hounds. Maybe you've heard of us. We look for all kinds of treasure."

Rose smiled. "And sometimes we even find some, like this coin." She took the doubloon from Captain Jib and handed it to Dixie. "Is this real?"

"Of course it's real," said Captain Jib, not waiting for Dixie to answer. "I've got a purse full of them myself, back at the house. The two here appraised my collection just last week, didn't you?"

"The captain's coins were genuine," said Dixie.

She returned the coin to Rose. "Yours is, too."

Alkali clapped his hands. "Then I was right. This is just like the *Whidah*!"

Captain Jib ran a hand through his beard. "The *Whidah*?" he said. "You mean old Sam Bellamy's schooner?"

"Why—why yes," said Alkali. "What do you know about Bellamy?"

"What don't I know?" said the captain. "I know all about the *Whidah*, how she crashed, and how the people out on Cape Cod scooped up her treasure like sea vultures."

"We're going to do the same thing," said Stanley. "We know where there's a wreck right here in Shadow Beach!"

"Stanley!" said Alkali. He lowered his voice. "That's supposed to be a secret."

Stanley scrunched up his shoulders and bit at his thumb. "Whoops, sorry," he said.

Alkali shrugged and turned to Captain Jib. "We think we may be on to something, but as of now it's only a theory."

"More than a theory, I'd say," said the captain. "Your doubloon is proof enough of that."

Captain Jib scratched at his beard some more. "So you call yourselves the Treasure Hounds, eh?"

"Yes, sir," said Stanley. "We're experts."

"You know, I, too, fancy myself an expert in the matter of lost and buried riches," said Captain Jib. He winked. "Perhaps we might be able to form a partnership. Share out your beach treasure with me, and I'll show you some special maps I've got."

"Maps?" said Alkali.

"Treasure maps," said the captain. He put a hand on Alkali's shoulder and led him and the other Hounds toward the front of the store, out of earshot of Dixie and Garth. "I'm talking inside information, mate, X-marks-the-spot kind of stuff."

"Sounds interesting," said Alkali.

"Real interesting," said Rose.

The captain looked over his shoulder as if afraid they were being spied on, then lowered his voice. "I know where a ship carrying one hundred million in gold and jewels went down." He lowered his voice further still. "I've got the maps that will lead us there. All I need is some young sea dogs like you to help me out."

Stanley whistled. "A hundred million dollars!" he said.

"So, what say you, mates?" said the captain. "Is it a deal? A share of yours for a share of mine?"

Alkali looked at Rose and Stanley and saw them both nod.

"All right," said Alkali. "Sure! It's a deal."

"Aye, that's the lad," said the captain. He smiled and shook Alkali's hand. "Come, we'll go to my house. I'll show you the maps."

"Looks like this is our lucky day," whispered Rose to Stanley.

"Sure is," replied Stanley. However, deep down he was worried that their luck was about to run out. If only he hadn't looked into that evil eye.

4

The Map

ON THE WAY TO CAPTAIN JIB'S HOUSE, the old sailor filled the Hounds' ears with tales of his many sea travels. It seemed he'd been most everywhere and seen most everything.

"Nearly eaten by cannibals in the Borak Islands," he said at one point. "They had me stuffed into a big pot. And if it hadn't been for some spices, that might have been the end of me."

"Spices?" said Rose.

"Hot peppers," said the captain. "The Borak chief loved spicy food, so he sent everyone off into the jungle to fetch some Borak red hots, the tangiest peppers on the island. The old fool. As soon as everyone was out of sight, I slipped my ropes and made my escape. He must have been pretty surprised when he came back and found his dinner had up and walked away."

Alkali laughed. "I wonder what everyone ended up eating that night?"

Captain Jib winked. "Hot-pepper soup, I would imagine."

"Here we are," said the captain as the group arrived at a small one-story house with an old rusty anchor in the front yard. "It's not often I have guests over," he added, unlocking the front door. "You'll have to excuse my quarters. I'm afraid you'll find them a little cluttered."

Cluttered was hardly the word for it! The Hounds had never seen a house as messy as the captain's. The rooms were a jumble of all manner of junk collected by the captain in his voyages. The walls of the living room were covered with wooden masks, and the floor was littered with travel magazines. Old fishnets hung from the ceiling, and boxes and sea chests were piled everywhere. The smell of seaweed hung in the air like an invisible fog.

"Follow me, lads," said the captain, signaling them to step into the next room. "There's treasure waiting!"

By the time the Hounds had caught up with Captain Jib, he had already found his map and was getting ready to spread it out on a large desk in the middle of a cluttered, but sunny, room.

"Here be our fortune, lads," said the captain. He licked his lips and unfurled the map. "Gather round, and I'll show you just where we'll hunt."

The Hounds crowded around the desk and stared at the map spread out before them. The captain's jade skull, still in its sack, anchored one side of the sheet of paper, and a hunk of red coral held down the other.

"These be the Florida Keys," explained the captain, pointing to a chain of small islands jutting out from the tip of Florida. "Many a ship has gone down in these waters, many a doubloon, too."

The Hounds were speechless. They'd never seen anything quite like the captain's treasure map.

"These are the Marquesas Keys," said the captain, running his finger down past the tip of the Florida Keys. "This is where, in 1622, a Spanish ship, the *Atocha*, carrying millions in gold and silver, went down in a terrible storm."

"The *Atocha*!" said Alkali.

"Aye, that was her name, all right," said the captain. "Right after she went down, the Spanish tried to salvage some of her cargo, but they found only a fraction of her treasure."

"Why, the *Atocha*'s a famous ship," said Alkali. "It's in the news all the time."

Captain Jib looked up from his map. "And right that it should be. Everyone's heard of her, but no one knows where she lies."

"But Captain—" said Alkali.

Captain Jib raised a finger to quiet Alkali and produced another map from a drawer in the desk. When he spread it out, everyone could see that it was a detailed study of the Marquesas Keys. Near one of the islands, in red ink, someone had drawn a big X.

"This is where the wreck lies," said the captain, pointing to the X. "I acquired this map just last year from an old print shop. The fools! They didn't know what they had."

Alkali cleared his throat. "Captain Jib," he said, "I think that maybe the print shop wasn't as stupid as you think."

The captain's head rose up out of the map like a ship's bow breaking through a wave. "What say you, lad?"

"That map isn't nearly as valuable as you might think, sir," said Alkali. "That treasure. It's already been found."

"Alkali!" said Rose. She drew back her head and wrinkled her brow. "What are you talking about?"

"Yes, explain yourself," said the captain angrily.

Alkali sighed. "The *Atocha* is the most famous wreck of our time," he said. "A group of divers have been working on it for years. So far they've found over a hundred and fifty million dollars' worth of gold and silver and jewels."

"I—I don't believe it," said the captain. He looked stunned. "Where did you hear about this?"

"Everywhere," said Alkali. "Don't you read the newspapers?"

Captain Jib shook his head. "Not in years," he said.

"I'm sorry," said Alkali. "I really am, but that treasure has already been found."

Captain Jib looked as if he had been struck by lightning. He collapsed into a big overstuffed chair and put his hand to the side of his face. "You must think me a silly old fool," he said.

"Not at all," Rose said sympathetically.

"How were you to know?" asked Stanley.

"Anyway, the treasure hunt's not over yet," said Alkali. "Remember, we've still got a wreck to explore. That gold doubloon I found didn't just fall out of the sky."

Captain Jib bit his lip. "I suppose this means our deal is off. If I can't share my treasure, I can't very well expect you to share yours."

"Not at all," said Alkali. "A deal is a deal. We want you with us tomorrow when we go after that wreck. You're an expert, Captain Jib. We'd be lost without you."

Captain Jib smiled. "You're very kind."

"We're serious," said Rose. "Will you join us?"

Captain Jib got out of his chair and clapped a hand on Rose's shoulder. "Mates through and through," he said. "I'd be honored to sign on with the Hounds."

"Great!" said Stanley.

"Wonderful!" said Alkali. "We have to put some equipment together, but we should be ready by tomorrow afternoon. Can you meet us at Brooks Street Beach at three?"

Captain Jib winked. "Three bells it is, lads. Captain Jib will be there. You can count on it."

5

Sharks at Sea

THE NEXT AFTERNOON, beneath a clear blue sky, the Treasure Hounds returned to Brooks Street Beach. They were eager to locate the wreck that Alkali believed was the source of his doubloon. To aid in the search, he and Rose brought their swim fins, masks, and snorkels; and Stanley brought along a pair of binoculars.

They hadn't been there long when Captain Jib, carrying a brass telescope, appeared at the top of the long stairs leading down to the sand.

"Ahoy, mates!" he crowed. "Treasure ho!"

"Good afternoon, Captain!" shouted Rose. "Come on down."

Before long, Captain Jib joined the others along the shore.

"I've brought my spyglass," he said, showing everyone his long telescope. "That way I can keep an eye on you in the water."

"And I brought my binoculars," said Stanley. "I plan to keep a lookout for sharks."

"Bah!" said Alkali, dismissing Stanley with a wave

of his hand. "We're not going to run into any sharks today."

"Don't be so sure," said Stanley. "Did you see the movie *Jaws*?"

Rose shook her head, then bent over and began pulling on her swim fins. "Stanley, when are you going to learn that not everything you see in the movies is real."

"Anyway," said Alkali, "sharks don't scare me. If one of those scaly creeps tries to bother us, I'll just bop him on the nose and send him packing, lickety-split."

"Sharks are no laughing matter," said Stanley, "especially in the summer when the water gets warm."

"Stanley is right about that," said the captain. "I've tangled with more than a few sharks in my day, and they're nothing to joke about."

"All right, then," said Rose, "how will we know if you see something?"

"If I see a fin cutting through the water, I'll start waving," Stanley said. He flapped his arms up and down like a seagull taking wing. "I'll go just like this."

Rose smiled and patted Stanley on the arm. "We'll be counting on you, so don't let us down."

"You two just find that wreck," said Captain Jib. "Stanley and I will do the rest."

Stanley made a fist and gave Rose a little punch on the shoulder. "Don't you worry, Rose. I won't let anything eat you and Alkali. That's a promise."

Alkali pulled on his swim fins and slipped on his mask. "Wish us luck," he said.

"Good luck," said Captain Jib.

"Be careful," warned Stanley.

As soon as Alkali and Rose had splashed into the ocean, Stanley and the captain climbed up onto some rocks so that they'd have a clear view of their friends.

The captain smiled. "It's good to be on a treasure hunt again," he said. "Sitting in that house of mine all day can sometimes get boring."

"I can imagine," said Stanley, "especially after all the adventures you've had."

While Stanley and the captain kept their eyes on the surface of the sea, Alkali and Rose scanned the bottom. Through their masks, the pair could clearly make out the rocky ocean floor. Occasionally they'd pass over an open stretch of sand littered with shells and small stones, and every now and then a lone fish, usually no more than a foot in length, would swim lazily by.

They were looking for any kind of pattern on the ocean floor. A line of what looked like rocks could be the shell-encrusted keel of a boat; lumps of round-ish rocks might be cannonballs; and anything shiny could be gold—the only metal that doesn't corrode in salt water.

They were both good swimmers, but they were careful to keep within fifty feet of shore, surfacing frequently to check on each other. Beyond that, the water was too deep to see the bottom anyway.

"What about those rocks down there?" asked Rose at one point.

"Nothing," said Alkali.

"There seems to be something twinkling behind

that seaweed," she said another time. "Could it be gold?"

Alkali dove down, and when he resurfaced he was holding the bottom of a broken bottle. "No luck," he said, dropping it back into the sea.

"Cannonballs!" said Rose, gesturing toward some roundish rocks on the ocean floor.

But an investigation proved that what she had seen was nothing but coral.

For half an hour, the two snorkeled through the water. Every few minutes Rose would glance back to shore, just to make sure Stanley and the captain were still keeping a lookout for them. Sharks weren't common in Shadow Beach, but they had been spotted before, big ones too, especially in summertime when the waters warmed up.

"We don't seem to be getting anywhere," said Rose, flipping up her mask. "Maybe we ought to go back in."

Alkali sighed and looked out to sea as he treaded water. "I can't believe there isn't something here," he said. "That doubloon had to have come from a wreck."

Rose smiled. She knew how much this treasure meant to Alkali. "All right," she said, "we'll look a little longer."

"Good," said Alkali, pointing toward the south. "We haven't checked over there yet. Follow me."

Rose took a breath and was about to stick her head under the water when something on the beach caught her attention.

"Alkali!" she said.

"What?"

She squinted toward shore. "Look at Stanley."

Alkali turned around and searched the shore for Stanley. When he finally picked him out, up on the rocks, he raised a hand and waved.

"Hello!?!" he called, though he knew his voice would never carry that far.

"Alkali!" said Rose. "Stanley isn't waving hello. He's sending us a signal." She glanced over her shoulder and shuddered. "He must have seen a shark!"

"Whoa, pardner," said Alkali. "Calm down." He turned around and scanned the horizon for a fin breaking through the waters, but he didn't see a thing. "What makes you think he's seen a shark?"

"That's the signal! Remember? He said if he saw anything, he'd wave his arms."

Alkali pulled off his mask and studied his friend in the distance. No doubt about it, he did seem excited about something. His arms were waving wildly, as if he were imitating a helicopter. As Alkali watched, Captain Jib got to his feet and began doing the same thing.

"Let's go," said Rose. Her voice was filled with fear. "Those two aren't just exercising."

"Maybe you're right," said Alkali. He looked out to sea once again. "Better to be safe than sorry."

Suddenly something brushed against Rose's leg. Normally she would have kept her cool head and figured it was a hunk of seaweed or a small fish, but now just one thing entered her mind: Shark! A man-eating shark had her number and was closing in for dinner!

"I felt him!" she screamed. "Shark! Help! Shark!"

Alkali's face went white as paste. Not even for a second did he consider bopping that killer fish on the nose, as he'd bragged he would. All he wanted to do just then was get to the beach, and get there fast.

Arms flailing like windmills, the pair cut through the water. They couldn't remember when they'd ever swum so fast or been so scared.

Rose thought of her mother. How sad she'd be when she got the news. "I'm sorry, Mrs. Flint," the policeman at the door would say. "Your daughter has been eaten up. She won't be home for dinner."

Rose would have cried if she could, but she couldn't. Every ounce of her energy was given over to the swim.

Now, a bit of seaweed brushed against Alkali's leg, and like Rose, he thought the shark was circling for the kill. Me and my stupid treasure, he thought, kicking wildly, hoping to scare off the invisible attacker. We're done for, and all for a few gold coins.

They both expected an attack at every second. But luck must have been with them because they never felt the shark's teeth. In minutes they reached the shore, exhausted, out of breath, and still shaken, but, happily, in one piece.

As they dragged themselves through the surf, Stanley and the captain hurried across the beach to meet them.

"Wow," said Stanley, "I've never seen you two swim so fast. You ought to try out for the Olympics."

Rose pulled herself up onto all fours and fought to catch her breath. "You—you—you'd swim fast too

if you had a shark on your tail," she said, gulping in bits of air between the words.

"Shark?" said Stanley. He slapped the side of his face with his hand. "Didn't I tell you to be careful?"

"He was huge," said Alkali, sitting down, fighting for his breath.

"Huge, huh?" said the captain. "Did you get a good look at him?"

"I didn't need to. I felt him," said Alkali. He looked up at the captain and gave him a quizzical look. "Didn't you see how big he was?"

"I didn't see any sharks," said the captain.

"Me neither," said Stanley.

"What?" gasped Rose.

"We didn't see any sharks," repeated Stanley.

"But—but—" sputtered Rose, "what about the signal? You were waving your arms!"

Alkali got to his feet. "What is this, some kind of a joke?" he said angrily. "Stanley, before we went out, you said you'd wave your arms if you saw a shark. We saw you wave. So where was the shark?"

"There wasn't one," said Stanley.

Rose glared at Stanley. "This isn't very funny. You had us scared half to death."

"I didn't give you the signal for sharks," said Stanley. He flapped his arms up and down. "This meant sharks. What I did was this." He made his arms revolve in front of his body like a windmill.

"So what was that supposed to mean?" asked Rose. "Helicopter coming?"

"No, it was supposed to mean, 'Come in quick,' " said Captain Jib. "The lad and I saw something fishy going on up on the cliff." He pointed up the side of the rocky, brush-covered hill at the rear of the beach. "There's trouble afoot, mates."

"Trouble?" asked Alkali. "What kind of trouble?"

"We saw two people running through the brush up there," said Captain Jib. "They looked like they were trying to hide something."

"Like what?" asked Alkali.

"Like a big round pair of brass cymbals," said Stanley.

"You mean like Mr. Drabb's cymbals?" Rose asked.

"It certainly looked that way," said Stanley.

"There were two of them, and they were crashing through the brush as if a pack of hounds were on their tail," said the captain. "I put my glass on them just as they took those cymbals out of a big canvas bag, but before I could bring the pair into focus, they disappeared behind that big boulder up there."

Rose shaded her eyes and looked up the side of the cliff. A giant, two-story boulder was set into the cliff, about halfway up the hill.

"So you don't know who they were?" said Alkali.

"Never got a look at their faces," said the captain. "But I do know this: When they left the hillside they weren't carrying the cymbals."

"So then they must be hidden up there!" said Rose.

"That's the way I got it figured," said Captain Jib. He scratched at his beard for a spell, then winked. "If you ask me, this calls for a bit of research. What say we climb the hill, mates? See what we can see."

"You sure those people you saw are gone?" asked Alkali.

"I saw them leave myself," said Stanley. "Believe me, if I thought they were still up there, I'd be going for the police, not for a climb."

"I'm game," said Alkali. "Won't Drabb be surprised if we find those cymbals."

Rose looked up the hill and drew in a deep breath. "Let's just hope that the cymbals are all we find on that hill," she said.

"What do you mean by that?" asked Alkali.

"I mean let's make sure that those cymbal thieves don't come back and find us snooping around," she said.

"I'm with you on that," said Stanley. "I'm not interested in doing anything dangerous. I don't care if we see those crooks, but I don't want them to see me."

6

Sharks on Land

BY THE TIME ALKALI AND ROSE had gathered up their equipment and changed into sweat shirts and jeans, it was getting late in the day, and long shadows, like rivers of ink, had begun to flow down the cliff.

"Follow me, mates," said the captain, waving everyone ahead with his telescope. "I've found a trail leading up the hill. "Step lively, now. I'll point us the way."

The trail wasn't much more than a narrow cut between the short, tiny-leafed bushes that covered the hill. Maneuvering through the sharp-branched bushes was difficult. The stones along the trail didn't make things any easier, either. A missed step, a patch of loose gravel, or a slippery rock and one could easily tumble back down the cliff to the beach, unless a prickly branched bush stopped him first.

"Ouch!" cried Rose, brushing her hand against a spiny branch. "I'm beginning to think we're crazy for climbing this hill."

"You won't be saying that if we find Mr. Drabb's cymbals and get our pictures in the paper," said Stanley.

"I suppose," said Rose. "Still I—Ouch!" Another branch, another cut.

Slowly and painfully they worked their way up the hill till at last they drew alongside the giant granite boulder the captain had pointed out earlier.

"The last time we saw those two, they were around here somewhere," said the captain. "I suggest we fan out and see if we can't find those cymbals."

"Maybe they stashed them in a bush," said Stanley.

"Or buried them," said Captain Jib.

"Or hid them under some rocks," said Rose. She put her hands on her hips and looked around. It was growing darker by the minute. "If we don't find them fast, we'll have to come back tomorrow."

"We'll find them," said Captain Jib. "Just keep your eyes peeled for anything out of the ordinary." He rubbed his hands together and chuckled. "Aye, there's nothing like an old-fashioned treasure hunt, is there, mates?"

"No, sir," said Alkali. He could already see the headlines in the paper: TREASURE HOUNDS FIND STOLEN GOODS! CRIME SPREE SOLVED! BIG PARADE IN THEIR HONOR PLANNED FOR TODAY!

He might have kept on daydreaming had not an angry voice from the far side of the boulder suddenly jolted him back to reality.

"You bakehead! What do you mean, you lost the car keys?" It was a woman's voice—angry and loud.

"I said I'm sorry," came another voice, this one a man's.

"Bah!" came the woman's reply. "You're the most

incompetent nincompoop I've ever had the misfortune to hook up with."

"Please, keep it down," said the man. "You want someone to find us here?"

Captain Jib and the Treasure Hounds hustled quickly over to the boulder and pressed their backs against the stone.

"No one's seen us," said the woman. "Just hurry and find those keys. It's getting dark."

"Ow!" cried the man. "These bushes are sharper than cactus. Sometimes I wish we'd never found this hide-out when we came here on vacation last spring."

"It wasn't as if we actually found it," said his partner. "It was more like it found us, after that big landslide opened everything up."

"It's certainly been perfect for our operations," said the man. "No doubt about that."

"And no doubt about the fact that we're going to do a lot of walking if those car keys don't turn up," said the woman. "Would you please hurry up and find them."

Stanley reached into his back pocket and rubbed his good luck Indian bone. "Come on, baby," he whispered, "do your stuff. Get us out of this."

"I'm really getting worried," said the man again. "What if someone discovers us up here?"

"So what if they do? They won't be going anywhere." The woman cackled. "I'll personally fix them so that they never get off this hill. Don't you worry about that, my friend."

Stanley gulped and pressed himself against the

back of the rock. Not ten feet away evil people were plotting his own end.

"We've got to get out of here," he whispered. "These people sound dangerous."

"Aye, you're right about that," whispered the captain. "Not all sharks are found in the sea. That's for certain."

Rose looked about for a way to escape, but there was none. If they were to step out from behind the rock, they'd be spotted for sure, even in the dark. "We'd better stay here till they leave," Rose said quietly. "No telling what those crooks might do if they caught us."

"I agree," said Alkali softly. "Let's just hope they don't need to come around to this side of the boulder."

"Ahhhh! Oh, no! A spider!" said Stanley, suddenly slapping at his hand.

They all turned to glare at Stanley. "Shhhh!" they said together.

"Loo—loo—look!" gasped Stanley. His voice was quivering, and his finger, which was pointing down at his leg, was shaking. "We're standing on top of a nest of spiders. They're crawling on my legs!"

Rose looked down. Suddenly she, too, was gripped with a feeling of horror. The ground beneath their feet was alive with tiny red spiders! It looked like zillions of them!

A moment later, they were crawling onto Rose's jeans; Alkali's, too. Rose brushed off about a hundred of them and saw another hundred swarm right back

on. "I can't stand this," she said under her breath. "Let's just start walking. We have a right to be on this hill. We'll just say we're on a hike."

"They'd know we'd overheard them," said Alkali. "We can't take the risk." He reached down and swatted a bunch of spiders swarming around his ankle.

"I'm sorry, but I really hate spiders," whispered Stanley. He was dancing up and down, trying, unsuccessfully, to keep both his feet off the ground. "Let's get out of here."

"Nothing's going to mess up our operation now." It was the woman's voice again. "Anybody gets in our way . . . Blamo! Curtains!" She let out another horrible little cackle. "Know what I mean?"

"Read you loud and clear, dear," said her partner.

Stanley gulped. He read her loud and clear, too. Maybe the spiders weren't so bad after all. At least they didn't mean to harm him.

"Steady, lads," said the captain. "These spiders are harmless. They won't hurt us."

"You sure?" said Stanley skeptically.

"Aye, I'm sure," whispered the captain hoarsely. "Now, if these were the jungles of New Guinea and the spiders were green instead of red, well, then, we'd have something to worry about. But these? Mere overgrown gnats."

There was a rustle of brush on the other side of the boulder, and Captain Jib suddenly clammed up. Someone coughed, and everyone froze.

"I think I might have dropped them under this bush," said the man. "I wish I'd brought out the flashlight. I can barely see."

"Say, did you see that movie on TV last week, *Invasion of the Mutants*?" asked the woman. "You know, the one starring those big hairy spiders."

Stanley brushed a spider off his arm and shuddered.

"I really loved it when that swarm of spiders attacked the fisherman in the swamp," she continued. "And—and wasn't it great when they started crawling up his neck?"

"Oh, no," said Stanley. There were spiders under his pants legs now. "Please get out of here and stop with the *Invasion of the Mutants* talk."

"And, hey!" The man laughed. "What about when that purple one crawled into his ear! I thought I was going to die!"

Stanley closed his eyes and started counting slowly to himself. "Please stop, please," he whispered. "Please go away."

"Ah! I've got 'em. The keys were in my pocket all the time," said the man. "Isn't that something!"

"Noodle head!" said the woman. "Now, come on, let's get out of here before it's too dark to find our way."

"At last!" Stanley sighed. "They're leaving."

Captain Jib and the Hounds held their places and their tongues for a few more minutes. Then Captain Jib stuck his head out from behind the boulder and checked to make sure the coast was clear.

"They're gone," he said. "You can come on out."

The Hounds stepped quickly away from the boulder, sat down on the ground, and began brushing away the spiders.

"Of all the places to hide," said Rose.

"When they started talking about those big hairy spiders I thought I was going to pass out," said Stanley. He flicked a spider off the tip of his nose. "Bugs! Yuck! Who needs 'em!"

The captain put a finger to his lips. "Shhhh," he said. "They could come back."

"Who were those people, anyway?" asked Rose. "They were positively horrible."

"Their voices sounded familiar, but I can't recollect where I've heard them before," said the captain. "Might have been old sea mates of mine. I've sailed with some pretty rough characters in my day."

"Do you think those people were the ones who have been robbing everyone?" asked Stanley.

"I'd be willing to bet on it," said the captain. "Why else would they have had those cymbals?"

"We ought to go to the police," said Stanley.

"And tell them what?" said Rose. "That we heard some people looking for their car keys?"

"We need evidence," said Alkali.

"Alkali's right," said the captain. "Before we make our move against those two, we need to find out where those cymbals have been stowed."

"But what if they come back while we're snooping around?" asked Stanley. He wrapped his arms around his chest and shuddered. "That woman said it would be curtains for anyone she caught."

"She sure did sound mean," Alkali agreed.

"You said her voice sounded familiar, Captain Jib," said Rose. "Do you know who it could have been?"

"Maybe Shanghai Sally. She was pretty tough," said Captain Jib. "And she had that same horrible cackle. But, I don't know. I haven't seen her since the last time I was in China, some ten years ago."

"I bet it's somebody closer to home," said Rose. "Someone who knows this town and knows where everyone's valuables are!"

"You could be right," said the captain, "but we won't know for sure until we turn up those cymbals and have some evidence to hand over to the police."

Stanley gazed across the darkened hillside. "I think we should look for our evidence in the morning, when we've got some more light. This place is starting to give me the creeps."

"The lad's got a point," said Captain Jib. "You can't hunt for hidden goods in the dark. We'd be wasting our time."

"Then I say we meet back here in the morning," said Alkali. "Those cymbals aren't going anywhere overnight."

"Sounds okay," Rose agreed.

"Then it's a plan," said the captain. He started toward the top of the hill. "Lift anchor, lads! We'll resume the hunt tomorrow!"

7

Surprises

EARLY THE NEXT MORNING, Captain Jib and the Hounds gathered at the big boulder near where they'd seen the crooks carrying Mr. Drabb's cymbals.

"Those cymbals can't be far," said Alkali. "Look under every bush and stone till you turn them up."

"Let's look out for a cave opening, too," said Rose. "And if you see any broken branches, sing out."

"Broken branches?" said Stanley.

"Sure, so we know where the crooks have been," said Rose. "Indians used to track animals for miles that way."

"Mrs. Hartz sure taught you a lot about the Indians," said Alkali.

"I know Indian sign language, their smoke signals, even how to grind acorn meal," Rose said proudly. "I'm a real expert, I guess."

Stanley glanced nervously up the hill. "Enough about the Indians. Let's find that hiding place. I don't want to be here any longer than is necessary."

But finding the cymbals didn't prove to be easy. For the next half hour or so, Captain Jib and the Treasure Hounds picked their way across the sun-splashed hillside, peeking behind rocks, looking beneath bushes, and pulling back piles of tangled brush. They saw ants, plenty more spiders, and lots of bottles and cans. But all they got for their trouble were scratches on their arms and sweat on their brows.

After a while Rose climbed on a little rock and scanned the area, looking for a glint of brass or a pile of fresh dirt. But all she saw were her friends, their backs bent into the hillside as they searched under every bush and rock they saw.

"Maybe we're wasting our time," she said loudly. "Perhaps they didn't hide anything up here."

Captain Jib stood up and wiped his forehead with the back of his hand. "No, Rose. Stanley and I saw them carrying those cymbals onto this hill. But when they left the cymbals were nowhere in sight."

"Maybe they picked them up when they returned for those car keys," said Rose.

"That could have been," said Alkali. "We never saw them come or go."

"If we don't get out of here soon, we could be in big trouble," said Stanley. "Let's not forget what those two said they'd do to anyone they caught snooping around."

"Those two don't scare me," said Alkali bravely. "Let's keep looking, at least a little longer."

"You can look all you want," said Stanley. He swung around a little rock and started across a small, grassy clearing. "I'm calling it quits. It's time we admitted that we're just wasting our time."

Rose bent down and leaped from the rock. "Maybe Stanley's right," she said.

"Sure I am," said Stanley. "In fact ninety-nine percent of the time if you would just listen to— Ahhhh!"

Rose looked up when she heard Stanley's scream. But her friend was nowhere in sight. All she saw was Alkali, looking very surprised.

"Stanley disappeared!" cried Alkali. "He fell into a hole. Right over there!"

"Quickly!" said Captain Jib, hurrying toward the place Alkali had pointed to. "The lad's in trouble!"

"Heavens!" Rose gasped as she ran to join Alkali and Captain Jib in the little clearing.

Sure enough, Stanley had fallen into a hole—a pretty big one, too. It was about four feet deep and had been disguised with brush and grass, most of which was now scattered around Stanley, who sat at the bottom, rubbing his head.

Rose got down on her hands and knees and looked into the hole. A short wooden ladder was propped against one of the dirt walls, and attached to its side, hanging by a nail, was a silver flashlight. "Stanley," she asked, "you okay?"

Stanley opened an eye and stared up into the bright sunlight. "Am I okay? I just fell down a giant hole. How can I be okay?"

"Are you hurt?" asked Alkali, coming up alongside Rose.

Stanley stretched out his arms and twisted his head around. "I guess I didn't break anything, though I sure am sore." He reached into his back pocket and pulled out the whalebone. "Ouch! No wonder I'm hurting. I landed right on this."

"Your lucky teeth," said Alkali with a smile.

Stanley snorted. "Yeah, some luck." He rubbed his back and pulled himself to a seated position. "Tell me, what kind of an idiot would cover a hole like this anyway?"

Rose rolled her eyes. "Stanley, you sure you're all right? Who do you think would do something like this?" Rose could almost see the light bulb blink on in Stanley's head.

"Oh, I get it," he said. He glanced around and saw a tunnel leading out of the base of the pit. "This is the hide-out we've been looking for."

Alkali tapped his head. "Good thinking, Stanley."

"Stanley, a flashlight's hanging on the ladder. Shine it into the hole and tell us what you see," said Rose.

Stanley wasn't sure he cared to find out what was lurking in that dark cave, but he did as he was told.

"Wow," he said, after switching on the light. "There's a regular cave in there. It's huge." He glanced up at Captain Jib and the Hounds. "I'm going inside. The room looks big enough to stand up in."

Captain Jib and the Hounds watched as Stanley pushed himself through the narrow opening at the bottom of the hole. Once he was inside, Rose climbed down the ladder and peered into the cave entrance.

"Anything in there?" she asked.

"I'll say," said Stanley. "Wow! Hurry up, you guys. You've got to get down here and take a look at this."

A few moments later, everyone had come down the ladder and crawled into the cave.

"Oh, my," said Rose, looking at the dimly lit contents of the cave.

"I can't believe it!" gasped Alkali.

"Seeing is believing," said Captain Jib, shaking his head. "I have a feeling the police are going to be very interested in what we've found here."

No doubt about that. For what Stanley had discovered was a vast storehouse of stolen goods. Arranged along the rough rock and dirt walls of the cave were all kinds of valuables.

"Why, look, it's 'The Wreck of the *Mary Rose*,'" said Captain Jib, pointing to a huge, gold-framed painting of a ship being torn apart by a storm. "That used to hang in the home of my old shipmate Billy Barnes. I remember him telling me it was pinched just last week."

"And look at all these jewel boxes," said Alkali. He bent down and opened a silver and gold box. "Whoa, Nellie! It's full of rings and necklaces."

"And that old clock against the wall," said Rose. "That belongs to Mrs. Bailey, one of our neighbors. She had it appraised last month and told my mother it was worth a small fortune."

"Eeeeyahhh!" screamed Stanley, jumping back from a box he'd just opened. "It's that giant purple spider we saw the other day at the Hammerhead Art Appraisers. Yuck!"

As Stanley backed away from the bug, he bumped into something on the floor. Clang! Stanley nearly jumped a mile. He gasped when he saw what he'd tripped on. "Mr. Drabb's cymbals!" he cried.

"And—and—and—" stammered Captain Jib. He crossed the cave and picked up a small leather pouch. "By barnacles! It's my own coin purse!" He emptied

the contents of the purse into his hand, and out spilled a dozen or so gold doubloons. They looked just like the one Alkali had found on the beach.

"Incredible!" said Rose. "Who knew you had those?"

Alkali snapped his fingers. "Wait a minute!" he exclaimed. "How did the thieves know about any of the things in here?"

"Of course! The appraisal service!" said Rose. "I'll bet all of the stuff in here passed through that shop."

"Now I know why those voices sounded so familiar," said Captain Jib. "They belonged to Dixie and Garth."

"Why, the nerve!" said Rose.

"They weren't stupid. That's for sure," said the captain. "They set up that business and then waited for the unsuspecting citizens of Shadow Beach to bring their most valuable items right to them."

"And remember how they asked clients where they kept their stuff?" said Rose. "'I hope you've got it stored in a safe place,' they'd say. 'I keep it in the closet,' said the lady with the spider."

"And I told them about my doubloons!" cried Captain Jib. He stared down at the coins in his hand. "They played me for a fool, no doubt about that."

"We'll see who plays the fool in the end," said Alkali. "Once the cops find out about this, Dixie and Garth are going to have a lot of questions to answer."

"We ought to take some of these things out so we can show them to the police," said Stanley. "I don't think it would be wise to hang around here any longer than we have to."

"Uh, oh," said Captain Jib. He'd been busily counting his coins. "There are only thirteen doubloons here. I should have fourteen."

"Are you sure you counted right?" asked Rose.

"I'm positive," said the captain. "One's definitely gone, lost or stolen for sure and certain."

Alkali reached into his pocket and drew out his doubloon. "I'll bet this is yours," he said. "Garth or Dixie probably spilled your bag of coins while coming down the hill. And the one I found must have rolled all the way to the beach."

"Maybe," said Captain Jib, "but how to prove it?"

"There's no shipwreck off Shadow Beach," said Alkali. "We proved that yesterday." He held out his hand. "This has to be yours. It looks just like the rest."

"I couldn't accept it, Alkali, but I must admit I'm in a ticklish situation here," said the captain. "I can't very well go on holding thirteen coins. It's an unlucky number."

"Captain Jib, don't be silly," said Rose. "There's no reason why having thirteen coins should be unlucky. It's just a dumb old superstition, like that skull of yours. The one you said had an evil eye—" Suddenly, Rose put a hand to her cheek. "Oh, no!" she exclaimed. "Your skull! Dixie and Garth know you have it!"

"And where I have it, too!" said the captain. Even in the dim light, the Hounds could see his eyes flash with anger. "Those low-down sea dogs! They've probably got their mitts sunk into my old sea chest this very instant!"

"Then let's not waste any more time," said Alkali. "We'll grab a few of those jewel boxes as evidence and get out of here on the double."

"We've got to hurry," said Rose. "Let's scoot."

Captain Jib slipped the doubloons into his pocket, Alkali picked up a pair of jewel boxes, and Stanley, wasting no time, headed for the cave opening.

Double-quick, he was back at the entrance and out into the warm summer sunlight.

"I'll see you all on top," he said, starting up the ladder. "Let's hurry."

"We're right behind you, pal," said Rose.

Stanley climbed the short ladder and was about to boost himself out when he found himself staring into a pair of black leather boots.

"Uh, oh," he said. Cranking his head up, he discovered the boots had legs in them, legs belonging to none other than slick-haired Garth, the appraiser. Stanley gulped, then gulped again when he saw what Garth had tucked under his arm.

"Uh, oh!" he said again. "It's Captain Jib's jade skull. And it's out of the sack!"

Despite his better judgment, Stanley found himself staring into the skull's big red eye. It seemed as though that big ruby was winking at him.

"I'm done for," he said. "Cursed by the evil eye."

"So you're one of those Treasure Hounds we met the other day!" said Garth. He smiled, showing off a set of perfectly polished white teeth, as he reached down to grab Stanley's arm. "Let me help you out of there, young fellow. You and I better have ourselves a little talk."

8

Into the Darkness

FOR ONCE, Stanley didn't freeze. He knew just what to do. "Yikes!" he screamed and slid down the ladder as if it were a fire pole. He landed in the pit with a thud. "Run for your lives!"

Rose was on her hands and knees, having just come out of the cave when Stanley let out his yell.

"What's wrong?" she gasped.

"It's—it's them!" he said, pointing up at the sky. "Back in the cave!"

Rose didn't have to wait for any further explanation. She dove back through the opening, tumbled over once, then turned around in time to see Stanley come shooting in right behind her.

"Who was it?" asked Alkali. The flashlight in his hand cast a shadow across his face that made his eyes look like round, empty black sockets.

"It was Garth!" said Stanley. "Captain Jib, he had your jade skull!"

"The dog!" said the captain. "Was he alone?"

"You bonehead! You let them get away!" came a high, scratchy voice from somewhere outside.

"Sounds like Dixie's along, too," said Rose.

Stanley looked at Alkali, then back at Rose, then over at Captain Jib. "What are we going to do?"

"Where's that flashlight, lunkhead?" It was Dixie again. "The kids must have taken it. Good thing I brought this one from the car. Now, let's go in there and drag them out. Idiot! This is all your fault."

Alkali quickly cast his eyes about the room for something they could use to defend themselves. "We outnumber them four to two," he said. "Maybe we can make a stand in here."

"Aye, that's a tempting thought," said the captain, "but not a very wise plan. Those two could be armed. We have no idea."

"And I'm not interested in finding out, either," said Stanley.

"Me neither," said Rose.

Alkali quickly looked around the cave. There were only two openings. One went out the front and was the same opening that Dixie and Garth were about to come through. It would hardly do. The only other choice was down the narrow passageway that led to the back of the cave.

Alkali shone the light into the tunnel and took a deep breath.

"Anybody up for a little cave exploring?" he asked.

"Not really," said Stanley.

"We could get lost back there forever," said Rose.

"Or be buried in a cave-in," said Stanley.

"Don't you worry, Dixie. I won't let those kids get away again," said Garth. It sounded as though he was just outside the cave.

"I'm not worried," replied Dixie, "because I'll get

them if you don't." She let out another one of those blood-curdling cackles, then added, "*I'll* make certain those kids never get out of here. Ever!"

"Then into the tunnel it is!" said Stanley, quickly overcoming his fear of cave-ins. "Hurry, let's go! They might have weapons."

"I'm right behind you," said Rose, no longer worried about getting lost.

Alkali pointed the flashlight down the tunnel and led everyone into the hillside. "Follow me," he said. "With a little luck we'll get out of this yet."

Ha! A little luck, thought Stanley, jogging along behind Alkali and Rose. If we'd had a little luck, we wouldn't be in this mess right now.

Eerie shadows, like giant bats, flitted across the walls as Captain Jib and the Treasure Hounds made their way through the rocky tunnel. At times the passageway would narrow so much that they had to turn sideways to pass through. Then, just when it looked as though it might dwindle to nothing, it would open into a small room. Occasionally they'd pause at one of these places to catch their breath, but usually they'd just hurry through without so much as a look one way or the other. That was because Dixie and Garth were never far behind, and their voices echoed constantly through the chambers of the cave.

"Just follow those footprints!"

"This way!"

"They can't be far now!"

Every once in a while the tunnel would branch. Alkali usually picked the wider passageway, but not always.

"Those two are stuck on us like ticks," said Alkali at one point. "If only we could shake them."

"They're following our footprints," said the captain. "If only there were a way to disguise our steps."

"Not in this soft dirt," said Rose. "Our only hope is to lose them some way—get them to make a wrong turn."

On they plunged, ever deeper into the mountain, down one rocky tunnel after another, always just a step or two ahead of their pursuers.

"We're never going to find our way out of here," said Stanley. "This place is like a maze."

"Just keep moving, lad," said Captain Jib. "There's no turning back now."

If Stanley had any doubts about the truth of Captain Jib's words, they were dispelled soon enough when Dixie yelled, "You can't escape your fate, Treasure Hounds. We're closing in. The end is near!"

Stanley lowered his head, quickened his pace, and along with everyone else hurtled deeper into the cave.

At last, however, the tunnel led them into a big, high-domed cavern from which there appeared to be no exit. As Alkali stood in the middle of the cavern and searched the walls with the light for a way out, he slowly felt his throat begin to tighten with fear.

"We're in for it now," he said. "This looks to me like the end of the line."

"It's a lot more than that," whispered Rose. She looked nervously down the passageway and then took the flashlight from Alkali and pointed it up at the ceiling. "Look, the walls are covered with Indian pictographs."

Sure enough, when Rose let the light play slowly across the walls, a colorful panorama of pictures came into view. There were drawings of fish and spears, of Indians wearing long capes and fancy headdresses. There was a drawing of an archer shooting at the moon, and over the tunnel entrance, a fistful of bent arrows being held up to the sun by a tall Indian warrior.

"This is an incredible discovery. This must be where Stanley's whalebone came from," said Rose. "Mrs. Hartz said that Indian pictographs in this area are very rare." She pointed to a series of drawings showing fish rising out of the sea and flying toward a full moon. "This tells the story of a great Indian fisherman. It's all about how he talked the fish right out of the waters and into the tribe's pots."

"You really do read Indian writing well," said Alkali. "I bet you'll get an A in Mrs. Hartz's class."

"Rose isn't going to get any grade if Garth and Dixie catch us," whispered Stanley. "In case you haven't noticed they're closing in."

"Stanley's right," said Captain Jib. "Dixie and Garth can't be far behind us."

Dixie's words, echoing loudly down the passageway, indicated they were, indeed, quite near.

"What do you mean the batteries are getting weak?" they heard her shout. "You jolterhead, why didn't you buy new ones when you had the chance?"

"Sounds like their light is getting dim," whispered Rose. "If it goes out before they find us, maybe we can still escape."

"Turn off the light so they can't see us," said Cap-

tain Jib. "Perhaps we can catch them by surprise and jump them before they have a chance to harm us."

Rose switched off the flashlight, and the cave was plunged into the most complete blackness any of them had ever experienced. It was scary, but not nearly so frightening as the faint light that soon appeared at the far end of the tunnel when Garth and Dixie rounded the final bend in the passageway.

"Uh, oh," whispered Rose. "Here they come."

The Hounds pressed themselves against the back wall of the cave and waited and watched as the dim yellow light got closer and closer.

"Just look at that light!" complained Dixie. "Another five minutes and it's going to be out. You fool, what then?"

"We'll use the kids' flashlight," said Garth. He gave a nasty laugh. "After we're done with them, they won't need it anyway."

"If we find them," said Dixie. They had arrived at the entrance to the cavern. In the dim light they couldn't see Captain Jib or the Treasure Hounds. Had they listened carefully, though, they probably could have heard the Hounds' hearts beating.

Stanley reached into his back pocket and pulled out his lucky teeth. He wasn't going down without a fight.

Neither was Rose. She tightened her grip on the flashlight and raised it over her head.

"Hey, look, it's another big room," said Garth, shuffling forward. "Shine the light over here so I can see."

When Dixie swung the flashlight around, she caught

a glimpse of the only thing her dim light was capable of picking up, the brightest, whitest object in the room, Stanley's lucky teeth, which he was holding high above his head.

"What the—!" she gasped.

"A skull!" screamed Garth, making the same mistake Stanley had made three days earlier.

Realizing that the teeth were all they could see, Stanley began wagging them up and down, making them appear to be floating freely about the room.

"It's—it's coming for us!" said Garth desperately. He began backing away.

"That thing doesn't scare me!" shouted Dixie. She raised her hands over her head and seemed to be ready to charge. "I'll fix that bag of bones. Stand back!"

Rose couldn't let her come forward. Without hesitation, she hurled the flashlight at Dixie, missing the woman's head by inches.

The sight of something zooming out of the black so startled Dixie that she leaped backwards, hit her head against the wall, and was knocked out cold. Her light clattered to the ground and blinked out for good.

The room went black again. Garth's shouts and screams filled the air.

"The skeleton. It's loose! It's loose! Save me, please!" Garth sounded as if he'd gone nuts.

Stanley chuckled to himself and slipped the teeth back into his pocket. "Maybe these choppers are lucky after all," he murmured.

"Light! Light! Rose, get the light!" It was Alkali's voice.

"I can't," said Rose. "It's gone. I threw it at Dixie. It's probably smashed into a hundred pieces by now."

Stanley felt his heart sink. They were goners. Without a flashlight they'd never find their way out. They were doomed, all right. Even with the flashlight, getting out would have been difficult, considering the way the passageways had so often twisted and turned and divided. Without the light it would be hopeless.

"What do we do now?" asked Captain Jib from somewhere in the pitch-black room.

"Rose, I can't believe you threw away our only light," cried Alkali. "Do you know what that means?"

Stanley answered for her. "It means we're finished."

"No, it doesn't," came Rose's voice. "Come over here, all of you. I've got a plan."

Rose kept up a steady stream of chatter till she felt first Captain Jib, then Alkali and Stanley approach her. "Take my hand," she said to Stanley. "Alkali, you take Stanley's hand, and Captain Jib, grab hold of Alkali. We're getting out of here."

"Wa—wa—wait!" Garth's voice came out of the inky void. "You can't leave me here with that thing. Please take me with you."

"Sorry, not on this trip," said Rose. "But just sit tight. We'll be back in a little bit for you and Dixie."

"Bu—bu—but the monster!" he cried.

Rose led her friends along the wall and back into the tunnel. Just as they started to shuffle down the corridor, Dixie apparently came to.

"Hey! What happened to the lights?" she cried.

When Garth's answer didn't quite satisfy her, she launched into a string of accusations and insults that went on for at least five minutes, maybe longer, but by then the Hounds were out of earshot.

Each time Rose arrived at a spot where the tunnel branched, she took the passageway to the left.

"Rose," said Stanley, "do you really think you can guess your way out of here?"

"What if we're going in circles?" said Alkali. "We might end up back where we started—with Garth and Dixie." Alkali shuddered.

"And the skeleton." Stanley laughed.

"You fellows will just have to trust me," said Rose.

Alkali sighed. "I hope you know what you're doing."

Me, too, said Rose to herself.

For what seemed like hours, they crept through the narrow black passageways, always keeping to the walls, always bearing to the left, always straining their eyes for a glimpse of the cave entrance.

The tunnel branched, then branched again, and all at once Rose smelled a whiff of salt air. They turned another corner, slipped down a narrow passageway, and suddenly Alkali began to shout. "Light! Light! I see light."

Sure enough, there was a faint glow at the end of the tunnel. Now they were running for the light as if it were a pile of gold coins. A moment later, they were in the room with the stolen goods, and a moment after that they were outside, shielding their eyes against the bright sun and letting the fresh air fill their lungs.

Alkali put an arm on Rose's shoulder and gave her a hug. "That was incredible. How did you do it?"

"All I was doing was following instructions," said Rose.

"Instructions? From whom?" asked Captain Jib.

"From an Indian in one of those pictographs," explained Rose. "The one who was holding the fistful of bent arrows. Remember him?"

"Sure," said Stanley. "Above the tunnel entrance."

"I was hoping that it meant follow the tunnel to the left, the way the arrows were bent, and you'll find the sun," said Rose.

Captain Jib put an arm on Rose's shoulder and gave her a little hug. "Aye, you're a genius, Rose. Positively brilliant."

"Not me," she said. "The Indians. They're the ones we should thank."

Stanley looked back into the cave and chuckled. "I guess we'd better go for the police. We can't very well leave Dixie and Garth in there forever."

"I just hope they have the sense to stay put," said Rose. "I'd hate to see them get lost."

"Anyway, it's all out of our hands now," said Captain Jib. "From here on out, this is a matter for the police. Why, what's this?" he said, suddenly spying his jade skull beneath a bush. "Garth must have dropped it here after he saw you, Stanley."

"I'll get it," said Rose. She bent and and picked it up.

"Careful now," said Captain Jib. He averted his eyes so as not to see the skull. "Don't look into the ruby, Rose. It's bad luck, you know."

"Captain Jib, I told you I don't believe in that kind of stuff," said Rose.

"Neither did Garth and Dixie," said the captain,

"and just look what happened to them. They're heading for a long spell of bad luck, probably about ten years' worth, in the county jail."

"Hmmmm," said Rose. "That is something to think about, but I don't know. It's just not scientific."

"Take your chances," said Captain Jib.

"I guess I will," said Rose. And, trusting in science, she looked right into that big red eye one more time and winked.

9

Sharks on the Hook

CAPTAIN JIB CALLED THE POLICE, and five minutes later three police cars, their sirens wailing, roared out to the cliffs above Brooks Street Beach.

Sergeant Andy Long, a short, plump veteran of the force, bounded out of his car and quickly took charge.

"Captain Jib, are you the one who called about the stolen goods?" he asked.

"Yes, sir," replied the captain. "The Hounds and I think we've just put an end to the crime spree here in town."

Sergeant Long chuckled and hitched up his pants. "The crime spree? Listen, Jib, the department has been trying to put an end to those robberies for two months. We haven't made an inch of headway. Are you trying to tell me that you and these kids have solved the whole thing?"

Three policemen behind the sergeant put their hands to their mouths and tried to choke back laughs.

Rose glared at the officers and said, "We didn't call you out here on some wild goose chase. We've got plenty of proof. In fact, it's right under your feet."

Sergeant Long glanced down at the earth. "Huh?"

"The stolen goods, sir. They're in a cave," said Alkali. "And you're standing right on top of it."

"A cave, you say?"

"Aye, and quite a sight I think you're going to see there," said Captain Jib. He waved to the police. "Follow me, mates, and bring your flashlights! The booty you've been searching for is waiting."

The captain led the parade of Hounds and police down the cliff and into the cave.

"Watch your heads," cautioned Captain Jib, ducking through the low, narrow cave opening, "and turn your flashlights on. You'll find it's dark inside."

When Sergeant Long and the others saw the room full of stolen goods, they gasped.

"Well, I'll be," said the sergeant.

"Just look at it all!" said another police officer.

Sergeant Long shook his head. "It appears I had you folks pegged all wrong," he said. "This is quite a find you've made."

"Everything in this room has been stolen," said Rose. "We're almost certain of it."

"I don't doubt that," said the sergeant. He patted Rose on the shoulder. "When word about this gets out, you kids are going to be big heroes. You, too, Captain Jib. Tell me, how did you find this place anyway?"

"It's a long story," said Alkali. "We'll explain it all later, but there's more."

"More stolen goods?" said Sergeant Long.

"No, more to the story," said Rose. "We've captured the thieves."

"You have?" said Sergeant Long. "Tell me. Where?"

"Way in the back of this cave," said Alkali. "They're Garth and Dixie. You know, the two people who run the Hammerhead Art Appraisers."

"I know exactly who they are," said Sergeant Long. "They've been doing a lot of business, I understand."

"And a lot of stealing, too, as you can see," said Captain Jib.

"If you'll follow the footprints that lead back into the hillside, you'll find them waiting at the end of the tunnel," said Rose. "But be careful. They could be dangerous."

"I'll take my best officers," said Sergeant Long. "I don't think we'll have any trouble."

Forty-five minutes later, when Sergeant Long and his men got to the end of the tunnel, Garth was so happy to see them he practically leaped into their arms.

"We're saved!" he yelled as soon as he saw the approaching flashlights. "I knew they'd come back for us."

"Saved?" snorted Dixie a few moments later. "You cabbagehead, it's the police!"

"So it is, ma'am," said Sergeant Long. "I'm afraid we'll have to take you two in on suspicion of robbery."

"Robbery?" said Dixie. "What are you talking about?"

"I'm talking about all the goods in the front of the cave," said the sergeant.

Dixie glared at Garth. "Nincompoop! This whole thing is your fault."

"My fault?" cried Garth. "Wait a minute. This was your idea, not mine."

"You were the one who did the actual stealing," said Dixie. She pointed an accusing finger at Garth. "You were the one who broke into the homes."

"Not true!" gasped Garth. "You came along half the time. Dixie, you're not only a thief, you're also a liar."

"Oh, yeah, well who was the one who—?"

"Whoa, whoa!" ordered Sergeant Long. He held up a hand for silence. "We'll settle this argument later, before the judge. Now come on, you two, let's go."

10

Heroes

WHILE SERGEANT LONG AND HIS MEN were bringing out Garth and Dixie, word spread through Shadow Beach that the thieves responsible for all the recent robberies had been cornered. Before long the cliff above Brooks Street Beach was filled with citizens anxious to see the crooks arrested. It seemed that everyone had come out for the show, including some reporters from the *Shadow Beach Times*. Even the mayor was there, and so was Rose's teacher, Mrs. Hartz.

"Someone told me you found some pictographs in that cave," said Mrs. Hartz the moment she spotted Rose.

"She sure did," said Stanley. "And she read them, too. That's how we got out."

"A discovery like this could make you famous," said Mrs. Hartz. "Rose, you've made me very proud."

Rose blushed. "If you hadn't taught me how to read those symbols, the Hounds and I might still be trapped inside that cave."

Suddenly a shout went up from the crowd. Sergeant Long and his men had just emerged from the cave,

Garth and Dixie in tow. A few moments later, the police brought the pair to Captain Jib and the Hounds for final identification.

"These the ones?" asked Sergeant Long.

Dixie and Garth glared at the Treasure Hounds as if somehow they could scare them into clamming up. But Captain Jib wasn't intimidated by the nasty looks. Not one bit.

"Aye, those are the sea snakes, all right," he growled. "Stole my doubloons, they did, and my skull as well."

"And my painting!" said an old lady in a pink dress. She waved her fist in the air.

"And my jewelry!" said another lady, pushing her way through the crowd.

"And what about my gold-headed cane?" shouted a red-faced man, wagging a finger at Dixie.

"And my cuckoo clock!" yelled someone else.

"And my diamond earrings!"

Dixie and Garth didn't look as though they cared to argue with the crowd. As soon as Sergeant Long opened the door to his squad car, the pair quickly jumped inside.

"Please, everyone," said Sergeant Long, raising a hand to quiet the crowd, "listen up! All your goods will soon be returned to you. The police are right now bringing them up from the cave."

A cheer went up from the crowd, but the sergeant quieted them once again. "If you want to applaud anyone, cheer Captain Jib and the Treasure Hounds. They're the ones who found your goods. They're the real heroes here today."

And before he could finish, a chorus of hoorays filled the air.

Captain Jib and the Treasure Hounds drank in the applause.

"This has been a great adventure," said Captain Jib. He slapped Alkali on the back and gave him a wink. "I haven't had this much fun in thirty years. Next time you go after a treasure, you let me know, all right?"

Alkali smiled and tipped back his cowboy hat. Then, giving Captain Jib a wink of his own, he said, "Captain Jib, any time you want to hook up with us, you're welcome. In fact, Stanley, Rose, and I have been talking, and if you have no objections, we'd like to make you an honorary Treasure Hound."

Captain Jib bit his lip. For a moment it looked as if he just might burst into tears. "I'm speechless," he said. "You couldn't have made me happier, mates."

The captain reached into his pocket and pulled out his coin purse. "And now I have something for you," he said, drawing two coins from the purse. "Since Alkali already has a doubloon, it's only fitting that Rose and Stanley have one, too." He presented the gold coins to the pair and added, "Now you're all honorary pirates."

"Wow!" said Stanley.

"We're speechless, Captain Jib," Rose said, smiling. "You couldn't have made us happier, mate!"

The next day Alkali's dreams came true. The town of Shadow Beach had a big parade down Main Street in honor of the new heroes. Captain Jib and the

Treasure Hounds, riding in the back seat of a red convertible, waved to all the townspeople as their car slowly passed by.

"This is great!" said Stanley, waving to his math teacher, Mr. Davis. "I feel just like a big star."

Pop! Pop! Pop! Flashbulbs exploded all around them. The next morning their pictures would be on the front page of the *Shadow Beach Times*, and the publicity was certain to bring them more business than they could ever handle.

Clang! The sounds of cymbals split the air.

Rose turned around and spotted Mr. Drabb. His precious cymbals in hand, he was proudly marching at the head of the entire symphony orchestra. Like everyone else, they'd turned out that day to honor Captain Jib and the Hounds.

Clang! He clapped his cymbals again and laughed. No doubt about it, Mr. Drabb was in a celebrating mood.

"Thank you all!" he shouted. "You don't know how happy you've made me."

Rose smiled. "How did you get your cymbals?" she asked. "Didn't the police keep them as evidence?"

"They let me borrow them for the parade," said Mr. Drabb. "Thanks again!"

"This sure has been a grand adventure, all right," said Captain Jib, smiling.

Clang! Clang! Clang! The cymbals rang out again, louder than ever.

"And this," said Rose, gesturing behind her at the parade, "is what I call the adventure's perfect grand finale."

Some Real Treasures for You to Find

HOWDY, PARDNER! I'm Alkali Jones and before the Hounds and I say good-bye we'd like to leave you with a little bonus. In the story you just read, perhaps you recall how I talked about two old treasures I'd read about, the Vienna, Idaho, Silver Hoard and the Wreck of the *Whidah*. Well, these are real treasures that have yet to be fully recovered. In the next two pages you'll find brief descriptions of the treasures and notes on where they might be found. Begin your search, though, in your local library. There, you will find all kinds of books on treasure and treasure hunting. Who knows, maybe someday you'll be a Treasure Hound, too. Good Luck!

THE WRECK OF THE WHIDAH

IN 1717, THE AMERICAN PIRATE Sam Bellamy captured a cargo ship by the name of the *Whidah* and began sailing her down the Massachusetts coast. The *Whidah*, loaded with gold and ivory, was quite a prize, but it was apparently too much ship for Bellamy's pirate crew to handle. On April 26, 1717, he rounded Cape Cod, and somewhere near Wellfleet Harbor, ran aground. Local residents, hearing of the disaster, flocked to the beaches and salvaged a great deal of the ship's goods that washed ashore. However, none of the ivory or gold was found, and it is believed to remain with the wreck to this day.

VIENNA SILVER HOARD

NOT MUCH REMAINS TODAY of the old mining town of Vienna, Idaho, except a few hunks of wood and a great deal of rusting tin cans distributed in dumps throughout the woods. But somewhere amid all that junk lies most of the profits from one of the town's saloons. The owner of the saloon is said to have buried his money near his business late one fall just before mining operations there shut down for the winter. Like most of the townspeople, he then left Vienna before the first snows could fall. Unfortunately, he died over the winter, and the location of his hoard, most of which is believed to be in silver, has never been found. Treasure hunters who have searched for the saloonkeeper's hoard have reported that the tin cans and rubbish in the area make searching with a metal detector extremely difficult. The site of what was once Vienna is located in Blaine County, Idaho. For the precise location, consult old maps as well as books such as *Idaho Treasure Tales and Treasure Trails*, by Jack Cubit and T.R. Glenn, published in 1968 by Alturas Enterprises in Boise, Idaho.